Bravo Phonics

Cecilia Chan

Level 1

The Commercial Press

Edited by: Betty Wong

Cover designed by: Cathy Chiu

Typeset by: Rong Zhou

Printing arranged by: Kenneth Lung

Bravo Phonics (Level 1)

Author:	Cecilia Chan
Publisher:	The Commercial Press (H.K.) Ltd.
	8/F, Eastern Central Plaza, 3 Yiu Hing Road, Shau Kei Wan, H.K.
	http://www.commercialpress.com.hk
Distributor:	THE SUP Publishing Logistics (H.K.) Ltd.
	16/F, Tsuen Wan Industrial Building, 220-248 Texaco Road,
	Tsuen Wan, NT, Hong Kong
Printer:	Elegance Printing and Book Binding Co., Ltd.
	Block A, 4/F, Hoi Bun Industrial Building 6 Wing Yip Street,
	Kwun Tung Kowloon, Hong Kong

© 2023 The Commercial Press (H.K.) Ltd.

First edition, First printing, July 2023

ISBN 978 962 07 0619 6

Printed in Hong Kong

Bravo Phonics Series is a

special gift to all children –

the ability to READ ENGLISH

accurately and fluently!

ENID!

ENJOY!

....

This book belongs to

_____

....

About the Author

The author, Ms Cecilia Chan, is a well-known English educator with many years of teaching experience. Passionate and experienced in teaching English, Ms Chan has taught students from over 30 schools in Hong Kong, including Marymount Primary School, Marymount Secondary School, Diocesan Boys' School, Diocesan Girls' School, St. Paul's Co-educational College, St. Paul's Co-educational College Primary School, St. Paul's College, St. Paul's Convent School (Primary and Secondary Sections), Belilios Public School, Raimondi College Primary Section, St. Clare's Primary School, St. Joseph's Primary School, St. Joseph's College, Pun U Association Wah Yan Primary School and other international schools. Many of Ms Chan's students have won prizes in Solo Verse Speaking, Prose Reading and Public Speaking at the Hong Kong Schools Speech Festival and

other interschool open speech contests. Driven by her passion in promoting English learning, Ms Chan has launched the Bravo Phonics Series (Levels 1-5) as an effective tool to foster a love of English reading and learning in children.

To all my
Beloved Students

Acknowledgement

Many thanks to the Editor, JY Ho, for her effort and contribution to the editing of the Bravo Phonics Series and her assistance all along.

Author's Words

The fundamental objective of phonics teaching is to develop step-by-step a child's ability to pronounce and recognize the words in the English language. Each phonic activity is a means to build up the child's power of word recognition until such power has been thoroughly exercised that word recognition becomes practically automatic.

Proper phonic training is highly important to young children especially those with English as a second language. It enables a child to acquire a large reading vocabulary in a comparatively short time and hence can happily enjoy fluent story reading. By giving phonics a place in the daily allotment of children's activities, they can be brought to a state of reading proficiency at an early age. Be patient, allow ample time for children to enjoy each and every phonic activity; if it is well and truly done, further steps will be taken easily and much more quickly.

Bravo Phonics Series has proven to be of value in helping young children reach the above objective and embark joyfully on the voyage of learning to read. It consists of five books of five levels, covering all the letter sounds of the consonants,

short and long vowels, diphthongs and blends in the English language. Bravo Phonics Series employs a step-by-step approach, integrating different learning skills through a variety of fun reading, writing, drawing, spelling and story-telling activities. There are quizzes, drills, tongue twisters, riddles and comprehension exercises to help consolidate all the letter sounds learnt. The QR code on each page enables a child to self-learn at home by following the instructions of Ms Chan while simultaneously practising the letter sounds through the example given.

The reward to teachers and parents will be a thousandfold when children gain self-confidence and begin to apply their phonic experiences to happy story reading.

Contents

About the Author	ii
To all my Beloved Students	iv
Acknowledgement	v
Author's Words	vi
Initial Consonant Sounds	1
s	2
f	6
h	10
t	14
p	18
m	22
n	26
r	30

Quizzes	35		
Quiz 2.1	36	Quiz 2.5	40
Quiz 2.2	37	Quiz 2.6	41
Quiz 2.3	38	Quiz 2.7	42
Quiz 2.4	39	Quiz 2.8	43

3 Vowel Sounds   45

Short 'a'   46
Short 'o'   50
Short 'i'   54

4 Drills   59

Drill 4.1   60
Drill 4.2   61
Drill 4.3   62
Drill 4.4   63
Drill 4.5   64
Drill 4.6   65

Drill 4.7   66
Drill 4.8   67
Drill 4.9   68
Drill 4.10   69
Drill 4.11   70

5 Initial Consonant Sounds   73

b   74
c   78
d   82
l   86

Quizzes	**91**
Quiz 6.1	92
Quiz 6.2	93
Quiz 6.3	94
Quiz 6.4	95

Drills	**97**
Drill 7.1	98
Drill 7.2	99
Drill 7.3	100
Drill 7.4	101
Drill 7.5	102

Quick Guide

 **Say**

SCAN ME

Scan

 Circle

Final Consonant Sounds   105

p, n, t, m

Revision	115
Revision 9.1	116
Revision 9.2	118
Revision 9.3	120
Revision 9.4	122

Answer Key   125

 Write    **Colour**    **Spell**

Hello, this is Ms Chan. How are you?
Are you ready to learn Bravo Phonics?
Let's learn about Consonant Sounds!

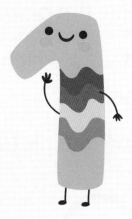

Initial Consonant Sounds

s   p

f   m

h   n

t   r

S

 Say the names of the pictures.

 Write the sound with which each picture begins on the line.

 Say the names of the pictures after me.

S

_____

_____

_____

_____

_____

2

Write the sound 's'.

 Say it aloud as you write it.

S s   S s

 Now colour the pictures.

S

Say the names of the pictures.

Circle those pictures that begin with the sound 's'.

S

S

 Say the names of the pictures with the sound 's' after me.

 Now colour the pictures with the sound 's'.

Say the names of the pictures.

Write the sound with which each picture begins on the line.

Say the names of the pictures after me.

f _____

_____

Write the sound 'f'.

 Say it aloud as you write it.

F f F f

 Now colour the pictures.

Say the names of the pictures.

Circle those pictures that begin with the sound 'f'.

f

 Say the names of the pictures with the sound 'f' after me.

 Now colour the pictures with the sound 'f'.

h

 Say the names of the pictures.

 Write the sound with which each picture begins on the line.

 Say the names of the pictures after me.

h

10

Write the sound 'h'.

 Say it aloud as you write it.

H h H h

 Now colour the pictures.

h

Say the names of the pictures.

Circle those pictures that begin with the sound 'h'.

h

 Say the names of the pictures with the sound 'h' after me.

 Now colour the pictures with the sound 'h'.

Say the names of the pictures.

 Write the sound with which each picture begins on the line.

 Say the names of the pictures after me.

 t

_____

_____

Write the sound 't'.

 Say it aloud as you write it.

T t   T t

 Now colour the pictures.

Say the names of the pictures.

 Circle those pictures that begin with the sound 't'.

 Say the names of the pictures with the sound 't' after me.

 Now colour the pictures with the sound 't'.

p

 Say the names of the pictures.

 Write the sound with which each picture begins on the line.

 Say the names of the pictures after me.

p _____ _____ _____

_____ _____ _____

Write the sound 'p'.

 Say it aloud as you write it.

P p P p

 Now colour the pictures.

p

Say the names of the pictures.

Circle those pictures that begin with the sound 'p'.

p

p

 Say the names of the pictures with the sound 'p' after me.

 Now colour the pictures with the sound 'p'.

m

 Say the names of the pictures.

 Write the sound with which each picture begins on the line.

 Say the names of the pictures after me.

m

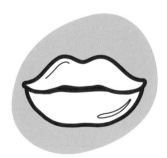

Write the sound 'm'.

 Say it aloud as you write it.

M m M m

 Now colour the pictures.

m

Say the names of the pictures.

Circle those pictures that begin with the sound 'm'.

m

24

m

 Say the names of the pictures with the sound 'm' after me.

 Now colour the pictures with the sound 'm'.

25

n

 Say the names of the pictures.

 Write the sound with which each picture begins on the line.

 Say the names of the pictures after me.

n

Write the sound 'n'.

 Say it aloud as you write it.

N n N n

 Now colour the pictures.

n

 Say the names of the pictures.

 Circle those pictures that begin with the sound 'n'.

n

NEWS

n

 Say the names of the pictures with the sound 'n' after me.

 Now colour the pictures with the sound 'n'.

r

 Say the names of the pictures.

 Write the sound with which each picture begins on the line.

 Say the names of the pictures after me.

r

_____   _____   _____

_____   _____   _____

Write the sound 'r'.

 Say it aloud as you write it.

R r   R r

 Now colour the pictures.

r

 Say the names of the pictures.

 Circle those pictures that begin with the sound 'r'.

 r

Are you ready for the Quizzes?
Let's start!

Quizzes

Quiz 2.1   Quiz 2.5

Quiz 2.2   Quiz 2.6

Quiz 2.3   Quiz 2.7

Quiz 2.4   Quiz 2.8

Say the names of the pictures.

Circle the correct sound with which each picture begins.

s t f h   t s f h   f h s t

s f h t   h t s f   h t s f

Now say the names of the pictures after me and check your answers.

Score
/6

Quiz 2.2

  Say the names of the pictures.

  Write the sound with which each picture begins on the line.

S
_____   _____   _____

_____   _____   _____

  Now say the names of the pictures after me.

Score

/6   37

Say the names of the pictures.

 Circle the word that matches each picture.

gun   ten   take

(sun)   hen   fake

fun   sen   snake

hat   hop   fire

sat   top   tire

fat   sop   hire

 Now say the names of the pictures after me and check your answers.

Score

/6

38

Quiz 2.4

 Say the names of the pictures.

 Spell the name of each picture by writing the sound with which the picture begins.

t ent _____and _____rog

_____ock _____op _____ead

 Now say the names of the pictures after me and check your answers.

Score

/6

39

Quiz 2.5

 Say the names of the pictures.

 Circle the correct sound with which each picture begins.

p m n r n m r p r p n m

r m n p p m r n m n p r

 Now say the names of the pictures after me and check your answers.

40

Score

/6

Say the names of the pictures.

 Circle the word that matches each picture.

pain
main
rain

rouse
mouse
house

nail
pail
mail

pest
nest
rest

mine
pine
nine

nose
rose
pose

 Now say the names of the pictures after me and check your answers.

Score

/6

41

Quiz 2.7

 Say the names of the pictures.

 Write the sound with which each picture begins on the line.

   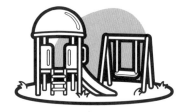   

_____   _____   _____

_____   _____   _____

  Now say the names of the pictures after me and check your answers.

Score

/6

42

Quiz 2.8

 Say the names of the pictures.

 Spell the name of each picture by writing the sound with which the picture begins.

_____ing   _____iano   _____oodles

_____urse   _____iger   _____ainbow

 Now say the names of the pictures after me and check your answers.

Score

/6

43

Let's learn about Vowel Sounds!

Vowel Sounds

Short 'a'

Short 'o'

Short 'i'

a

 Say the names of the pictures.

 Write the sound with which each picture begins on the line.

 Say the names of the pictures after me.

 a

_____ _____ _____

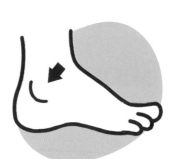

_____ _____ _____

Write the short sound 'a'.

 Say it aloud as you write it.

A a

 Now colour the pictures.

a

 Say the names of the pictures.

 Circle those pictures with the short sound 'a' in it.

cat

hat

a

cup

fan

bus

a

mango

pan

man

 Say the names of the pictures with the short sound 'a' after me.

 Now colour the pictures that have the short sound 'a'.

O

 Say the names of the pictures.

 Write the sound with which each picture begins on the line.

 Say the names of the pictures after me.

_____   _____   _____

_____   _____   _____

Write the short sound 'o'.

 Say it aloud as you write it.

O o O o

  Now colour the pictures.

O

 Say the names of the pictures.

 Circle those pictures with the short sound 'o' in it.

top

bat

O

box

sock

pig

 o

fox

lock

dot

 Say the names of the pictures with the short sound 'o' after me.

 Now colour the pictures with the short sound 'o'.

53

i

 Say the names of the pictures.

 Write the sound with which each picture begins on the line.

 Say the names of the pictures after me.

i

54

Write the sound 'i'.

 Say it aloud as you write it.

I i   I i

 Now colour the pictures.

Say the names of the pictures.

 Circle those pictures with the short sound 'i' in it.

pig

brick

i

octopus

six

wig

i

ring

pins

ankle

 Say the names of the pictures with the short sound 'i' after me.

 Now colour the pictures that have the short sound 'i'.

Are you ready for more practice?
Let's begin!

Drills

Drill 4.1   Drill 4.7

Drill 4.2   Drill 4.8

Drill 4.3   Drill 4.9

Drill 4.4   Drill 4.10

Drill 4.5   Drill 4.11

Drill 4.6

Say each sound along the line.

 Circle those that have the same sound as the first one.

s ⓢ f ⓢ p t ⓢ

f h t f n f f

h r p h a f h

t t m a t t r

a a a s m n a

 Now say the sounds after me.

Say each sound along the line.

 Circle those that have the same sound as the first one.

p s p n p t p

m h m m a f m

n r n h n n m

r r m r t s r

a f a a m a h

 Now say the sounds after me.

Say the sounds in each box.

Write the two letters together to form a new sound.

| s a | p a | f a | t a |
| sa | | | |

| f a | m a | n a | s a |
| | | | |

| h a | n a | r a | m a |
| | | | |

| t a | r a | p a | h a |
| | | | |

Now say the sounds after me.

Say each sound along the line.

 Circle those that have the same sound as the first one.

sa	(sa)	na	(sa)
	ha	(sa)	fa

fa	fa	na	ra
	ha	fa	fa

ha	sa	ha	pa
	ha	ha	ma

ta	ta	ta	sa
	na	ta	ta

 Now say the sounds after me.

Say each sound along the line.

 Circle those that have the same sound as the first one.

pa	ha	pa	pa
	ta	pa	sa
ma	pa	ma	fa
	ma	sa	ma
na	ta	na	na
	na	ma	na
ra	pa	ra	na
	sa	ra	ra

 Now say the sounds after me.

Say the sounds in each box.

 Write the two letters together to form a new sound.

s o	p o	f o	t o
SO			

f o	m o	n o	s o

h o	n o	r o	m o

t o	r o	p o	h o

 Now say the sounds after me.

SCAN ME

 Say each sound along the line.

 Circle those that have the same sound as the first one.

so	so	no	so
	ho	so	fo
fo	fo	no	ro
	ho	fo	fo
ho	so	ho	po
	ho	ho	mo
to	ro	to	so
	to	to	fo

 Now say the sounds after me.

Say each sound along the line.

 Circle those that have the same sound as the first one.

po	ho	no	po
	po	po	so
mo	po	mo	fo
	mo	mo	mo
no	to	no	no
	fo	mo	no
ro	ro	ro	no
	so	ro	ro

 Now say the sounds after me.

Say the sounds in each box.

Write the two letters together to form a new sound.

s i	p i	f i	t i
si	____	____	____

f i	m i	n i	s i
____	____	____	____

h i	n i	r i	m i
____	____	____	____

t i	r i	p i	h i
____	____	____	____

Now say the sounds after me.

Say each sound along the line.

 Circle those that have the same sound as the first one.

si	si	si	mi
	fi	si	hi
fi	ti	fi	fi
	hi	fi	fi
hi	si	hi	ti
	fi	hi	hi
ti	ti	si	ti
	ni	ti	fi

 Now say the sounds after me.

Say each sound along the line.

Circle those that have the same sound as the first one.

pi	mi	ni	pi
	pi	pi	si
mi	ti	mi	si
	mi	mi	hi

70

ni	ri	ni	ni
	ti	si	ni
ri	ti	mi	ri
	ri	ri	fi

 Now say the sounds after me.

Let's learn about Consonant Sounds!

Initial Consonant Sounds

b

c

d

l

b

Say the names of the pictures.

Write the sound with which each picture begins on the line.

Say the names of the pictures after me.

b

Write the sound 'b'.

 Say it aloud as you write it.

B b B b

 Now colour the pictures.

b

 Say the names of the pictures.

 Circle those pictures that begin with the sound 'b'.

b

 Say the names of the pictures with the sound 'b' after me.

 Now colour the pictures with the sound 'b'.

Say the names of the pictures.

 Write the sound with which each picture begins on the line.

 Say the names of the pictures after me.

C

_____ _____ _____

_____ _____ _____

Write the sound 'c'.

 Say it aloud as you write it.

C c C c

 Now colour the pictures.

C

Say the names of the pictures.

Circle those pictures that begin with the sound 'c'.

C

C

 Say the names of the pictures with the sound 'c' after me.

 Now colour the pictures with the sound 'c'.

d

 Say the names of the pictures.

 Write the sound with which each picture begins on the line.

 Say the names of the pictures after me.

d

Write the sound 'd'.

 Say it aloud as you write it.

D d D d

 Now colour the pictures.

d

 Say the names of the pictures.

 Circle those pictures that begin with the sound 'd'.

d

84

d

 Say the names of the pictures with the sound 'd' after me.

 Now colour the pictures with the sound 'd'.

Say the names of the pictures.

 Write the sound with which each picture begins on the line.

 Say the names of the pictures after me.

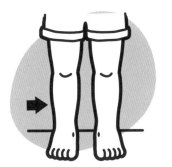

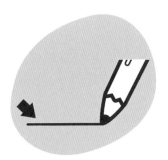

Write the sound 'l'.

 Say it aloud as you write it.

L l   L l

 Now colour the pictures.

Say the names of the pictures.

 Circle those pictures that begin with the sound 'l'.

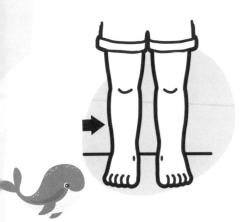

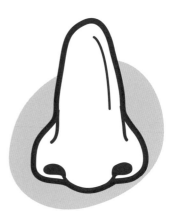

 Say the names of the pictures with the sound 'l' after me.

 Now colour the pictures with the sound 'l'.

89

Are you ready for the Quizzes?
Let's start!

Quizzes

Quiz 6.1

Quiz 6.2

Quiz 6.3

Quiz 6.4

Say the names of the pictures.

 Circle the correct sound with which each picture begins.

b c d l

d c l b

d c b l

c d l b

b c d l

d c l b

 Now say the names of the pictures after me and check your answers.

Score

/6

Quiz 6.2

 Say the names of the pictures.

 Write the sound with which each picture begins on the line.

_____ _____ _____

_____ _____ _____

 Now say the names of the pictures after me and check your answers.

Score

/6

93

Say the names of the pictures.

 Circle the word that matches each picture.

camp
(lamp)
damp

cat
mat
bat

map
lap
cap

cot
dot
lot

bee
see
fee

bow
cow
how

 Now say the names of the pictures after me and check your answers.

Score

/6

Say the names of the pictures.

 Spell the name of each picture by writing the sound with which the picture begins.

C___ap ___oat ___amp

___irty ___andle ___etter

 Now say the names of the pictures after me and check your answers.

Score /6   95

Are you ready for more practice?
Let's begin!

Drills

Drill 7.1

Drill 7.2

Drill 7.3

Drill 7.4

Drill 7.5

Drill 7.1

 Say each sound along the line.

 Circle those that have the same sound as the first one.

b   d   l   (b)   a   (b)   (b)

c   i   c   a   c   c   o

d   d   l   d   d   i   b

l   i   l   o   l   a   l

a   a   o   a   i   a   d

o   o   i   a   o   d   o

i   b   i   l   i   d   i

 Now say the sounds after me.

98

Say the sounds in each box.

 Write the two letters together to form a new sound.

b a **ba**	b o	b i
c a	c o	c i
d a	d o	d i
l a	l o	l i

 Now say the sounds after me.

Say each sound along the line.

 Circle those that have the same sound as the first one.

ba	ca	ba	da
	ba	la	ba
ca	da	ca	ca
	la	ca	ba
da	da	da	ba
	da	ca	la
la	ca	la	da
	la	la	ba

 Now say the sounds after me.

100

Say each sound along the line.

 Circle those that have the same sound as the first one.

bo	co	do	bo
	lo	bo	bo
co	bo	co	do
	co	lo	co
do	do	no	do
	co	do	lo
lo	co	lo	do
	lo	bo	lo

 Now say the sounds after me.

Say each sound along the line.

 Circle those that have the same sound as the first one.

bi	ci	di	li
	bi	bi	bi
ci	li	ci	bi
	ci	ci	di

di	di	li	di
	bi	di	di
li	bi	li	ci
	li	di	li

 Now say the sounds after me.

Let's learn more
Consonant Sounds!

Final Consonant Sounds

p

n

t

m

Final Consonant Sounds

 Say the names of the pictures.

 Write the sound with which each picture ends on the line.

t
_____   _____

_____

_____

_____

_____

_____

 Say the names of the pictures after me.

 Now colour the pictures.

Final Consonant Sounds

 Say the names of the pictures.

 Write the sound with which each picture ends on the line.

p _____   _____

_____

_____

_____

_____

_____

 Say the names of the pictures after me.

 Now colour the pictures.

Final Consonant Sounds

SCAN ME

 Say aloud the first sound.

 Circle one of the other sounds to build the word to match the picture.

 Write the word on the line.

ma (m (n) r)

man

pi (p n t)

_____

ha (l s t)

110

_____

pa (n m d)

_____

lam (b p r)

_____

ten (n m t)

_____

 Say the names of the pictures after me.

 Now colour the pictures.

Final Consonant Sounds

 Say aloud the first sound.

 Circle one of the other sounds to build the word to match the picture.

 Write the word on the line.

ba (t n r)

bat

_____

ca (a p o)

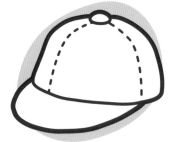

_____

pe (l a n)

_____

ma (s p o)

_____

ha (r m o)

_____

he (n p s)

_____

 Say the names of the pictures after me.

 Now colour the pictures.

Are you ready for more practice?
Let's begin!

Revision

Revision 9.1

Revision 9.2

Revision 9.3

Revision 9.4

Say the names of the pictures.

Write the sound with which each picture begins on the line.

_____   _____

_____

_____   _____

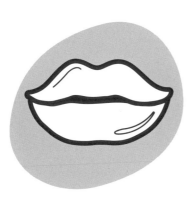

_____   _____

 Say the names of the pictures
after me.

 Now colour the pictures.

Revision 9.2

Say the names of the pictures.

Write the sound with which each picture begins on the line.

—————————   —————————

—————————

_____   _____

_____   _____

 Say the names of the pictures
after me.

 Now colour the pictures.

Revision 9.3

Say the names of the pictures.

Write the sound with which each picture begins on the line.

_____   _____

120

_____

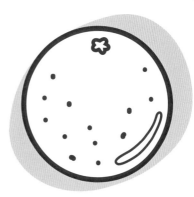

_____

_____

_____

_____

 Say the names of the pictures after me.

 Now colour the pictures.

121

Revision 9.4

Say the names of the pictures.

Write the sound with which each picture ends on the line.

_____   _____

_____

 Say the names of the pictures after me.

 Now colour the pictures.

Well done, students! You can check your answers with the Answer Key.

Answer Key

s

Say the names of the pictures.

Write the sound with which each picture begins on the line.

Say the names of the pictures after me.

S   S   S

S   S   S

Write the sound 's'.

Say it aloud as you write it.

S s   S s

S s   S s

S s   S s

Now colour the pictures.

2

3

s

Say the names of the pictures.

Circle those pictures that begin with the sound 's'.

s

Say the names of the pictures with the sound 's' after me.

Now colour the pictures with the sound 's'.

4

5

f

Say the names of the pictures.

Write the sound with which each picture begins on the line.

Say the names of the pictures after me.

f   f   f

f   f   f

Write the sound 'f'.

Say it aloud as you write it.

F f   F f

F f   F f

F f   F f

Now colour the pictures.

6

7

126

f

Say the names of the pictures.

Circle those pictures that begin with the sound 'f'.

f

Say the names of the pictures with the sound 'f' after me.

Now colour the pictures with the sound 'f'.

8

9

h

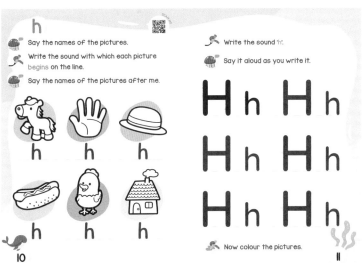

Say the names of the pictures.

Write the sound with which each picture begins on the line.

Say the names of the pictures after me.

h   h   h

h   h   h

Write the sound 'h'.

Say it aloud as you write it.

H h H h

H h H h

H h H h

Now colour the pictures.

10

11

h

Say the names of the pictures.

Circle those pictures that begin with the sound 'h'.

h

Say the names of the pictures with the sound 'h' after me.

Now colour the pictures with the sound 'h'.

12

13

127

t

🪼 Say the names of the pictures.

🐛 Write the sound with which each picture begins on the line.

🪼 Say the names of the pictures after me.

t   t   t

t   t   t

14

🐛 Write the sound 't'.

🪼 Say it aloud as you write it.

T t   T t

T t   T t

T t   T t

🐛 Now colour the pictures.

15

t

🪼 Say the names of the pictures.

⭕ Circle those pictures that begin with the sound 't'.

t

t

🪼 Say the names of the pictures with the sound 't' after me.

🐛 Now colour the pictures with the sound 't'.

16   17

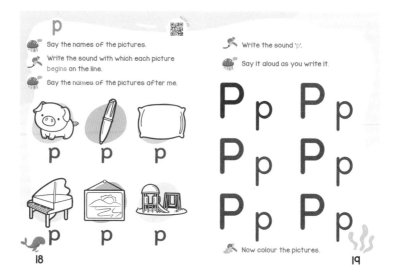

p

🪼 Say the names of the pictures.

🐛 Write the sound with which each picture begins on the line.

🪼 Say the names of the pictures after me.

p   p   p

p   p   p

18

🐛 Write the sound 'p'.

🪼 Say it aloud as you write it.

P p   P p

P p   P p

P p   P p

🐛 Now colour the pictures.

19

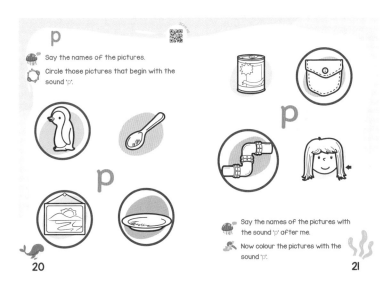

p

Say the names of the pictures.

Circle those pictures that begin with the sound 'p'.

p

p

Say the names of the pictures with the sound 'p' after me.

Now colour the pictures with the sound 'p'.

20

21

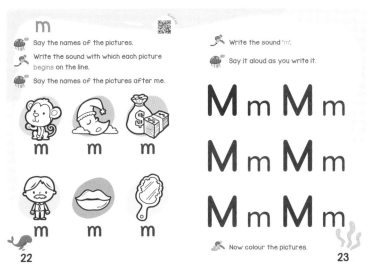

m

Say the names of the pictures.

Write the sound with which each picture begins on the line.

Say the names of the pictures after me.

m   m   m

m   m   m

Write the sound 'm'.

Say it aloud as you write it.

M m M m

M m M m

M m M m

Now colour the pictures.

22

23

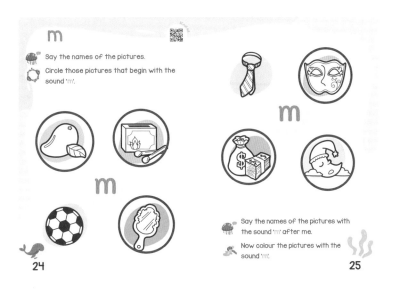

m

Say the names of the pictures.

Circle those pictures that begin with the sound 'm'.

m

m

Say the names of the pictures with the sound 'm' after me.

Now colour the pictures with the sound 'm'.

24

25

129

n

🪼 Say the names of the pictures.

🐛 Write the sound with which each picture begins on the line.

🪼 Say the names of the pictures after me.

n   n   n

n   n   n

🐋 26

🐛 Write the sound 'n'.

🪼 Say it aloud as you write it.

N n   N n

N n   N n

N n   N n

🐛 Now colour the pictures.

27

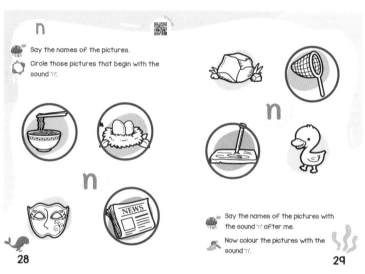

n

🪼 Say the names of the pictures.

⭕ Circle those pictures that begin with the sound 'n'.

n

n

🐋 28

n

🪼 Say the names of the pictures with the sound 'n' after me.

🐛 Now colour the pictures with the sound 'n'.

29

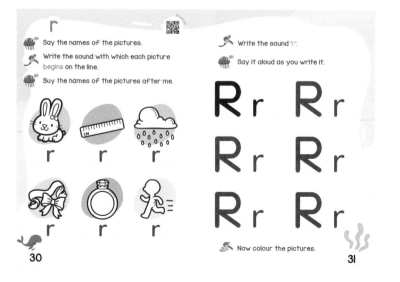

r

🪼 Say the names of the pictures.

🐛 Write the sound with which each picture begins on the line.

🪼 Say the names of the pictures after me.

r   r   r

r   r   r

🐋 30

🐛 Write the sound 'r'.

🪼 Say it aloud as you write it.

R r   R r

R r   R r

R r   R r

🐛 Now colour the pictures.

31

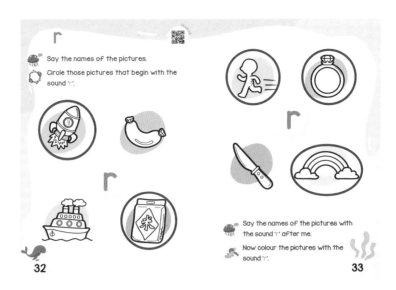

r

Say the names of the pictures.

Circle those pictures that begin with the sound 'r'.

r

r

r

Say the names of the pictures with the sound 'r' after me.

Now colour the pictures with the sound 'r'.

32

33

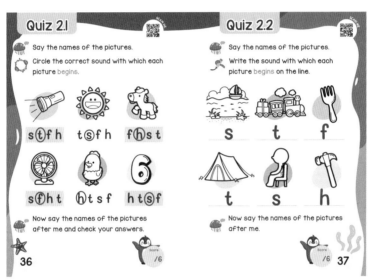

Quiz 2.1

Say the names of the pictures.

Circle the correct sound with which each picture begins.

s t f h   t s f h   f h s t

s f h t   h t s f   h t s f

Now say the names of the pictures after me and check your answers.

36

Score /6

Quiz 2.2

Say the names of the pictures.

Write the sound with which each picture begins on the line.

s   t   f

t   s   h

Now say the names of the pictures after me.

Score /6

37

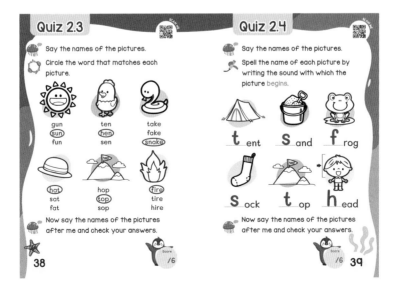

Quiz 2.3

Say the names of the pictures.

Circle the word that matches each picture.

gun   ten   take
sun   hen   fake
fun   sen   snake

hat   hop   fire
sat   top   tire
fat   sop   hire

Now say the names of the pictures after me and check your answers.

38

Score /6

Quiz 2.4

Say the names of the pictures.

Spell the name of each picture by writing the sound with which the picture begins.

t ent   S and   f rog

S ock   t op   h ead

Now say the names of the pictures after me and check your answers.

Score /6   39

131

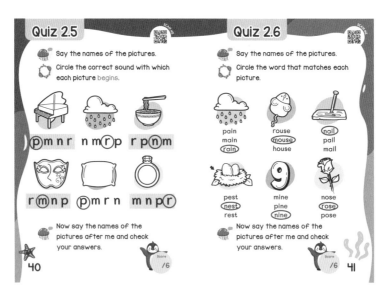

Quiz 2.5

Say the names of the pictures.

Circle the correct sound with which each picture begins.

(p) m n r n m (r) p r p (n) m

r (m) n p (p) m r n m n p (r)

Now say the names of the pictures after me and check your answers.

40   Score /6

Quiz 2.6

Say the names of the pictures.

Circle the word that matches each picture.

pain   rouse   (nail)
main   (mouse)   pail
(rain)   house   mail

pest   mine   nose
(nest)   pine   (rose)
rest   (nine)   pose

Now say the names of the pictures after me and check your answers.

Score /6   41

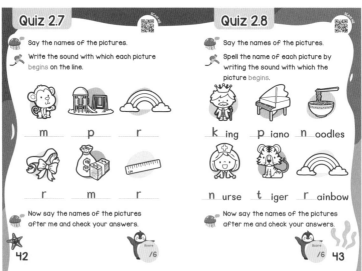

Quiz 2.7

Say the names of the pictures.

Write the sound with which each picture begins on the line.

_m_   _p_   _r_

_r_   _m_   _r_

Now say the names of the pictures after me and check your answers.

42   Score /6

Quiz 2.8

Say the names of the pictures.

Spell the name of each picture by writing the sound with which the picture begins.

_k_ ing   _p_ iano   _n_ oodles

_n_ urse   _t_ iger   _r_ ainbow

Now say the names of the pictures after me and check your answers.

Score /6   43

a

Say the names of the pictures.

Write the sound with which each picture begins on the line.

Say the names of the pictures after me.

a   a   a

a   a   a

Write the short sound 'a'.

Say it aloud as you write it.

Aa Aa

Aa Aa

Aa Aa

Now colour the pictures.

46   47

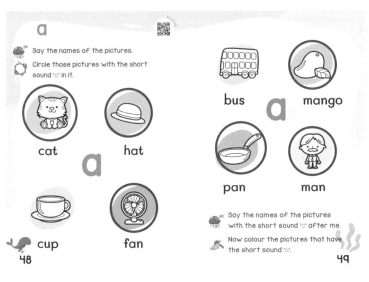

a

Say the names of the pictures.

Circle those pictures with the short sound 'a' in it.

cat hat a cup fan

48

bus a mango pan man

Say the names of the pictures with the short sound 'a' after me.

Now colour the pictures that have the short sound 'a'.

49

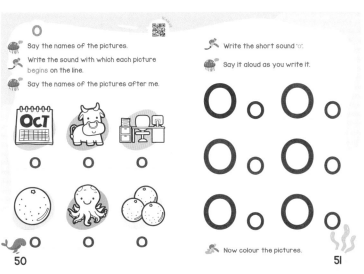

o

Say the names of the pictures.

Write the sound with which each picture begins on the line.

Say the names of the pictures after me.

O O O

O O O

50

Write the short sound 'o'.

Say it aloud as you write it.

O o O o

O o O o

O o O o

Now colour the pictures.

51

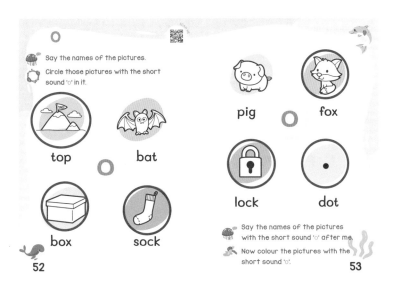

o

Say the names of the pictures.

Circle those pictures with the short sound 'o' in it.

top o bat box sock

52

pig o fox lock dot

Say the names of the pictures with the short sound 'o' after me.

Now colour the pictures with the short sound 'o'.

53

133

i

Say the names of the pictures.

Write the sound with which each picture begins on the line.

Say the names of the pictures after me.

i

i

i

i

Write the sound 'i'.

Say it aloud as you write it.

I i   I i

I i   I i

I i   I i

Now colour the pictures.

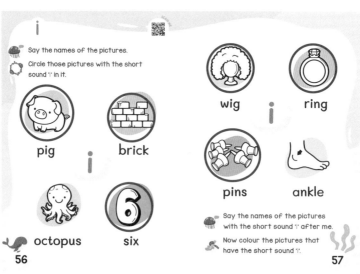

i

Say the names of the pictures.

Circle those pictures with the short sound 'i' in it.

pig

brick

octopus

six

wig   i   ring

pins   ankle

Say the names of the pictures with the short sound 'i' after me.

Now colour the pictures that have the short sound 'i'.

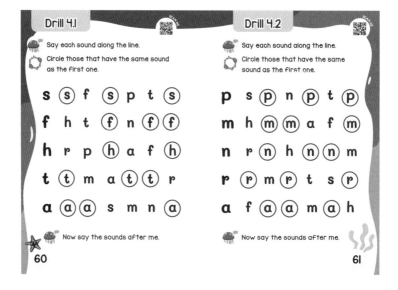

Drill 4.1

Say each sound along the line.

Circle those that have the same sound as the first one.

s (s) f (s) p t (s)

f h t (f) n (f) (f)

h r p (h) a f (h)

t (t) m a (t) (t) r

a (a) (a) s m n (a)

Now say the sounds after me.

Drill 4.2

Say each sound along the line.

Circle those that have the same sound as the first one.

p s (p) n (p) t (p)

m h (m) (m) a f (m)

n r (n) h (n) (n) m

r (r) m (r) t s (r)

a f (a) (a) m (a) h

Now say the sounds after me.

Drill 4.3

Say the sounds in each box.

Write the two letters together to form a new sound.

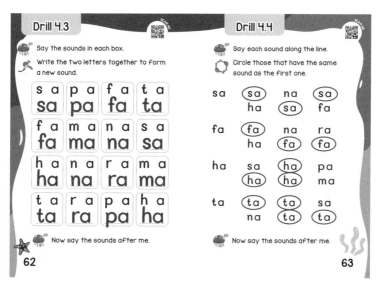

s a	p a	f a	t a
sa	**pa**	**fa**	**ta**

f a	m a	n a	s a
fa	**ma**	**na**	**sa**

h a	n a	r a	m a
ha	**na**	**ra**	**ma**

t a	r a	p a	h a
ta	**ra**	**pa**	**ha**

Now say the sounds after me.

62

Drill 4.4

Say each sound along the line.

Circle those that have the same sound as the first one.

sa (sa) na (sa)
        ha (sa) fa

fa (fa) na ra
        ha (fa) (fa)

ha sa (ha) pa
        (ha) (ha) ma

ta (ta) (ta) sa
        na (ta) (ta)

Now say the sounds after me.

63

Drill 4.5

Say each sound along the line.

Circle those that have the same sound as the first one.

pa ha (pa) (pa)
        ta (pa) sa

ma pa (ma) fa
        (ma) sa (ma)

na ta (na) (na)
        (na) ma (na)

ra pa (ra) na
        sa (ra) (ra)

Now say the sounds after me.

64

Drill 4.6

Say the sounds in each box.

Write the two letters together to form a new sound.

s o	p o	f o	t o
so	**po**	**fo**	**to**

f o	m o	n o	s o
fo	**mo**	**no**	**so**

h o	n o	r o	m o
ho	**no**	**ro**	**mo**

t o	r o	p o	h o
to	**ro**	**po**	**ho**

Now say the sounds after me.

65

Drill 4.7

Say each sound along the line.

Circle those that have the same sound as the first one.

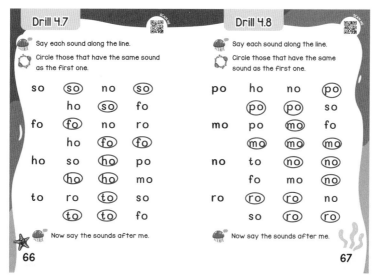

so (so) no (so)
        ho (so) fo

fo (fo) no ro
        ho (fo) (fo)

ho so (ho) po
        (ho) (ho) mo

to ro (to) so
        (to) (to) fo

Now say the sounds after me.

66

Drill 4.8

Say each sound along the line.

Circle those that have the same sound as the first one.

po ho no (po)
        (po) (po) so

mo po (mo) fo
        (mo) (mo) (mo)

no to (no) (no)
        fo mo (no)

ro (ro) (ro) no
        so (ro) (ro)

Now say the sounds after me.

67

135

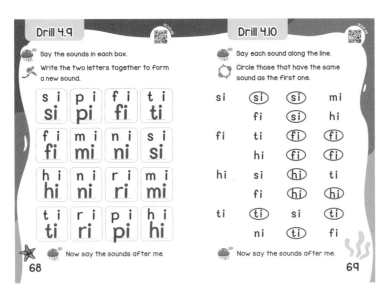

Drill 4.9

Say the sounds in each box.

Write the two letters together to form a new sound.

s i	p i	f i	t i
si	pi	fi	ti

f i	m i	n i	s i
fi	mi	ni	si

h i	n i	r i	m i
hi	ni	ri	mi

t i	r i	p i	h i
ti	ri	pi	hi

Now say the sounds after me.

68

Drill 4.10

Say each sound along the line.

Circle those that have the same sound as the first one.

si   (si)   (si)   mi
    fi   (si)   hi

fi   ti   (fi)   (fi)
    hi   (fi)   (fi)

hi   si   (hi)   ti
    fi   (hi)   (hi)

ti   (ti)   si   (ti)
    ni   (ti)   fi

Now say the sounds after me.

69

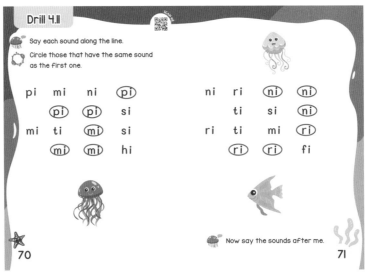

Drill 4.11

Say each sound along the line.

Circle those that have the same sound as the first one.

pi   mi   ni   (pi)
    (pi)   (pi)   si

mi   ti   (mi)   si
    (mi)   (mi)   hi

ni   ri   (ni)   (ni)
    ti   si   (ni)

ri   ti   mi   (ri)
    (ri)   (ri)   fi

Now say the sounds after me.

70

71

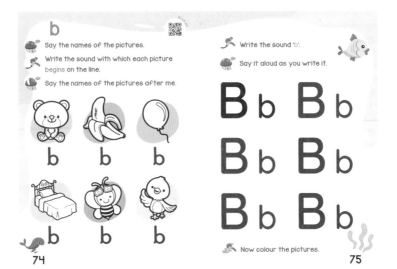

b

Say the names of the pictures.

Write the sound with which each picture begins on the line.

Say the names of the pictures after me.

b   b   b

b   b   b

Write the sound 'b'.

Say it aloud as you write it.

B b   B b

B b   B b

B b   B b

Now colour the pictures.

74

75

b

Say the names of the pictures.

Circle those pictures that begin with the sound 'b'.

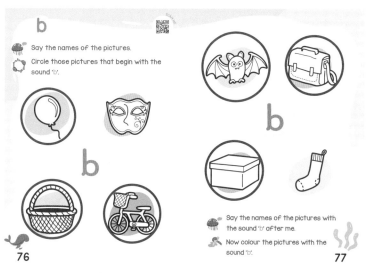

Say the names of the pictures with the sound 'b' after me.

Now colour the pictures with the sound 'b'.

76

77

c

Say the names of the pictures.

Write the sound with which each picture begins on the line.

Say the names of the pictures after me.

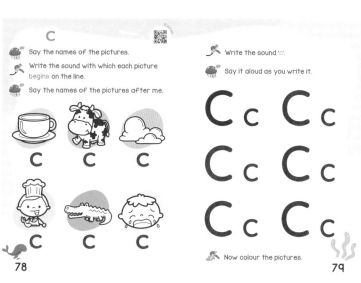

Write the sound 'c'.

Say it aloud as you write it.

Now colour the pictures.

78

79

c

Say the names of the pictures.

Circle those pictures that begin with the sound 'c'.

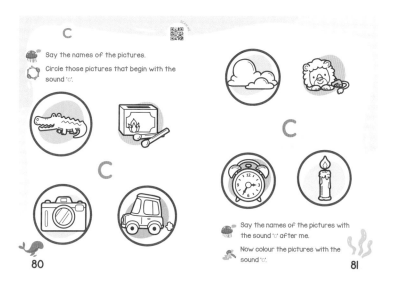

Say the names of the pictures with the sound 'c' after me.

Now colour the pictures with the sound 'c'.

80

81

137

d

Say the names of the pictures.

Write the sound with which each picture begins on the line.

Say the names of the pictures after me.

d   d   d

d   d   d

Write the sound 'd'.

Say it aloud as you write it.

D d   D d

D d   D d

D d   D d

Now colour the pictures.

82   83

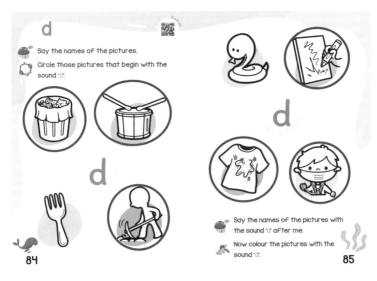

d

Say the names of the pictures.

Circle those pictures that begin with the sound 'd'.

d

Say the names of the pictures with the sound 'd' after me.

Now colour the pictures with the sound 'd'.

84   85

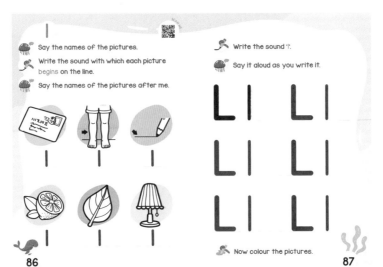

l

Say the names of the pictures.

Write the sound with which each picture begins on the line.

Say the names of the pictures after me.

l   l   l

l   l   l

Write the sound 'l'.

Say it aloud as you write it.

L l   L l

L l   L l

L l   L l

Now colour the pictures.

138

86   87

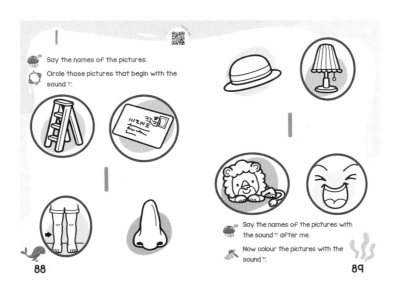

Say the names of the pictures.

Circle those pictures that begin with the sound 'l'.

Say the names of the pictures with the sound 'l' after me.

Now colour the pictures with the sound 'l'.

88

89

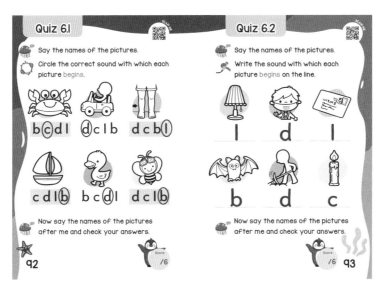

Quiz 6.1

Say the names of the pictures.

Circle the correct sound with which each picture begins.

b c d l   d c l b   d c b l

c d l b   b c d l   d c l b

Now say the names of the pictures after me and check your answers.

92   Score /6

Quiz 6.2

Say the names of the pictures.

Write the sound with which each picture begins on the line.

l   d   l

b   d   c

Now say the names of the pictures after me and check your answers.

Score /6   93

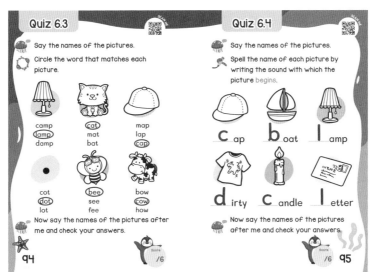

Quiz 6.3

Say the names of the pictures.

Circle the word that matches each picture.

camp   cat   map
lamp   mat   lap
damp   bat   cap

cot   bee   bow
dot   see   cow
lot   fee   how

Now say the names of the pictures after me and check your answers.

94   Score /6

Quiz 6.4

Say the names of the pictures.

Spell the name of each picture by writing the sound with which the picture begins.

c ap   b oat   l amp

d irty   c andle   l etter

Now say the names of the pictures after me and check your answers.

Score /6   95

139

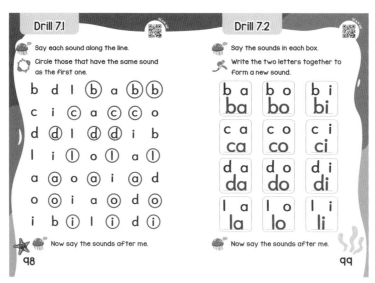

Drill 7.1

Say each sound along the line.

Circle those that have the same sound as the first one.

b   d   l   ⓑ   a   ⓑ ⓑ

c   i   ⓒ   a   ⓒ   ⓒ   o

d   ⓓ   l   ⓓ ⓓ   i   b

l   i   ⓛ   o   ⓛ   a   ⓛ

a   ⓐ   o   ⓐ   i   ⓐ   d

o   ⓞ   i   a   ⓞ   d   ⓞ

i   b   ⓘ   l   ⓘ   d   ⓘ

Now say the sounds after me.

98

Drill 7.2

Say the sounds in each box.

Write the two letters together to form a new sound.

b a **ba**	b o **bo**	b i **bi**
c a **ca**	c o **co**	c i **ci**
d a **da**	d o **do**	d i **di**
l a **la**	l o **lo**	l i **li**

Now say the sounds after me.

99

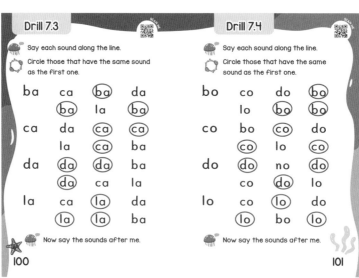

Drill 7.3

Say each sound along the line.

Circle those that have the same sound as the first one.

ba   ca   ⓑⓐ   da
  ⓑⓐ   la   ⓑⓐ

ca   da   ⓒⓐ   ⓒⓐ
  la   ⓒⓐ   ba

da   ⓓⓐ   ⓓⓐ   ba
  ⓓⓐ   ca   la

la   ca   ⓛⓐ   da
  ⓛⓐ   ⓛⓐ   ba

Now say the sounds after me.

100

Drill 7.4

Say each sound along the line.

Circle those that have the same sound as the first one.

bo   co   do   ⓑⓞ
  lo   ⓑⓞ   ⓑⓞ

co   bo   ⓒⓞ   do
  ⓒⓞ   lo   ⓒⓞ

do   ⓓⓞ   no   ⓓⓞ
  co   ⓓⓞ   lo

lo   co   ⓛⓞ   do
  ⓛⓞ   bo   ⓛⓞ

Now say the sounds after me.

101

Drill 7.5

Say each sound along the line.

Circle those that have the same sound as the first one.

bi   ci   di   li
  ⓑⓘ   ⓑⓘ   ⓑⓘ

ci   li   ⓒⓘ   bi
  ⓒⓘ   ⓒⓘ   di

di   ⓓⓘ   li   ⓓⓘ
  bi   ⓓⓘ   ⓓⓘ

li   bi   ⓛⓘ   ci
  ⓛⓘ   di   ⓛⓘ

Now say the sounds after me.

102

103

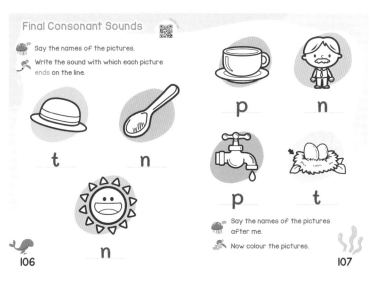

Final Consonant Sounds

Say the names of the pictures.

Write the sound with which each picture ends on the line.

t

n

n

p

n

p

t

Say the names of the pictures after me.

Now colour the pictures.

106

107

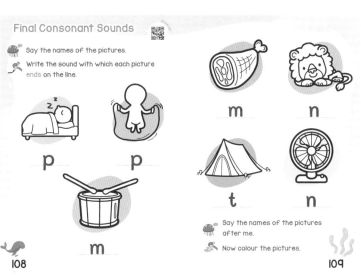

Final Consonant Sounds

Say the names of the pictures.

Write the sound with which each picture ends on the line.

p

p

m

m

n

t

n

Say the names of the pictures after me.

Now colour the pictures.

108

109

Final Consonant Sounds

Say aloud the first sound.

Circle one of the other sounds to build the word to match the picture.

Write the word on the line.

ma (m (n) r)

pi (p (n) t)

man

pin

ha (l s (t))

hat

pa ((n) m d)

lam (b (p) r)

pan

lamp

ten (n m (t))

tent

Say the names of the pictures after me.

Now colour the pictures.

110

111

141

Final Consonant Sounds

Say aloud the first sound.

Circle one of the other sounds to build the word to match the picture.

Write the word on the line.

ba (t n r)

bat

ca (a p o)

cap

pe (l a n)

pen

ma (s p o)

map

ha (r m o)

ham

he (n p s)

hen

Say the names of the pictures after me.

Now colour the pictures.

112

113

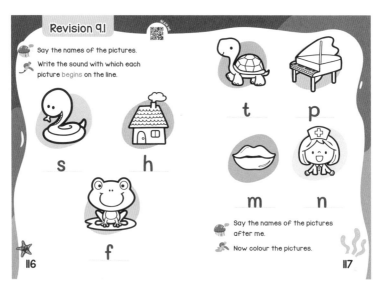

Revision 9.1

Say the names of the pictures.

Write the sound with which each picture begins on the line.

s

h

f

t

p

m

n

Say the names of the pictures after me.

Now colour the pictures.

116

117

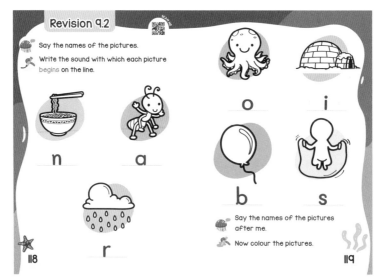

Revision 9.2

Say the names of the pictures.

Write the sound with which each picture begins on the line.

n

a

r

o

i

b

s

Say the names of the pictures after me.

Now colour the pictures.

118

119

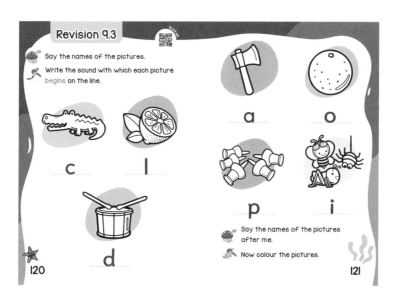

Revision 9.3

Say the names of the pictures.

Write the sound with which each picture begins on the line.

c

l

d

a

o

p

i

Say the names of the pictures after me.

Now colour the pictures.

120

121

Revision 9.4

Say the names of the pictures.

Write the sound with which each picture ends on the line.

p

n

t

n

p

m

t

Say the names of the pictures after me.

Now colour the pictures.

122

123

143